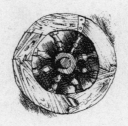

Rumpelstiltskin

Collect all the Everystories:

Rumpelstiltskin

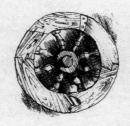

Retold by
Kit Wright

Illustrated by
Ted Dewan

■■SCHOLASTIC
Home of the Story

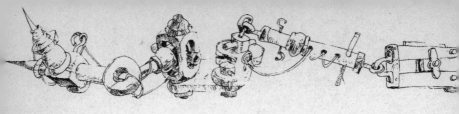

Scholastic Children's Books,
Commonwealth House, 1~19 New Oxford Street,
London WC1A 1NU, UK
a division of Scholastic Ltd
London ~ New York ~ Toronto ~ Sydney ~ Auckland
Mexico City ~ New Delhi ~ Hong Kong

First published by Scholastic Ltd, 1998

ISBN 0 590 11364 X

Printed by The Bath Press, Bath.

2 4 6 8 10 9 7

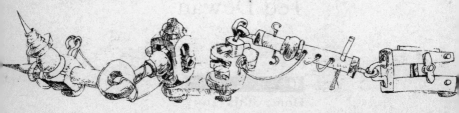

For Eddie Bonner

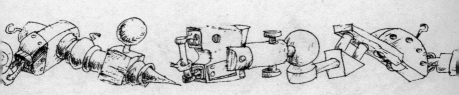

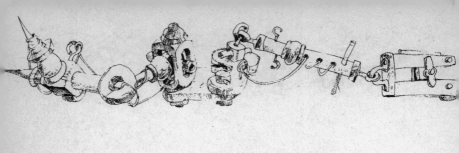

For Elsie Bonner

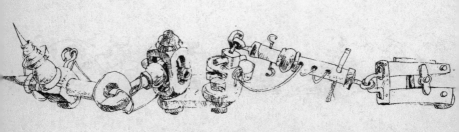

There was once an old miller who lived deep in the forest by a winding river. And he had a beautiful daughter named Isabella, whom he loved more than the breath in his body, more than his own life.

But the miller was poor.

Every day he sighed to himself, "If

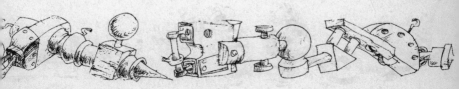

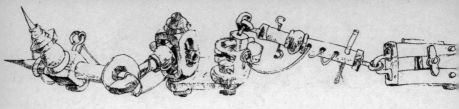

only I were a rich man, and could give Isabella the life of a fine lady!"

They both worked very hard at the mill, grinding the corn into meal to make bread. Round and round turned the huge wheel in the rushing water. Slowly inside the mill, the wooden cogs creaked, and the shaft spun, and the great stone went groaning round.

It was like an elephant dancing on the bank!

One day a Prince came riding through the forest. The sun shone through the canopy of the leaves, making a light like underwater. The birds sang and the Prince sang, for he was handsome and happy.

Then he came out of the trees and on to the river bank into broad sunlight. He reined in his horse and the tinkle of its harness died.

The only sounds were the water and the pounding of the mill.

But the Prince wasn't listening. He was looking.

For there stood Isabella, and she

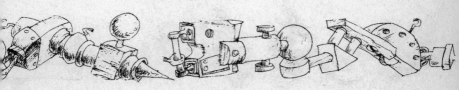

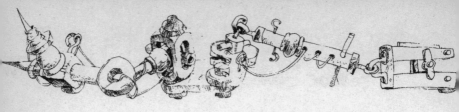

was the most beautiful sight the Prince had ever seen.

He swung down from his white horse.

"Beautiful lady, tell me who you are!"

"Why, I am Isabella, sir. My father is the miller."

And the Prince didn't have long to wait to meet him. Hearing them talk, he came running out. He was very jealous about his daughter, and didn't like her speaking to strange men.

"Who — "

And the miller's voice stopped in his throat. For the man standing in

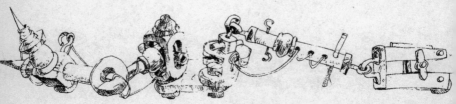

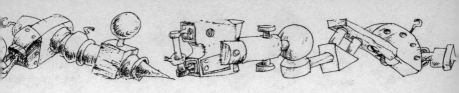

front of him was a Prince in all his majesty and finery.

"S-sir, forgive me!"

"Nothing to forgive, sir. Your daughter is the most beautiful girl in the world. That's what I wanted to tell her."

"Ah," said the miller. "Ah…"

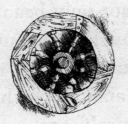

Now this is where he made his great mistake. The Prince had fallen in love

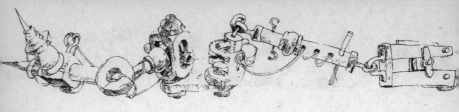

with Isabella the moment he saw her. He wanted to marry her. But the old man didn't know this.

Remember he loved his daughter more than the breath in his body, more than his own life. He wanted the very best for her, and this was a golden chance. So he said:

"She is not only beautiful, sir. She is clever enough to do anything."

"For instance?"

The old man racked his brains and he heard himself say:

"She can spin straw into gold!"

Then the Prince rode back on his white horse through the forest, with the leaves whistling against his arms and shoulders. In the Palace, there was the King.

"Fool of a boy! Where have you been?"

Well, the King was of course his father, and a very nasty old piece of work indeed. He was rich, richer than anyone, but not rich enough for himself. He wanted more.

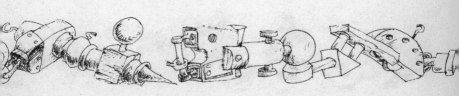

"Where have you been, fool of a boy?"
So the Prince told him.

"Father, I've been in the forest and down by the riverside. There I met the most beautiful girl in the world, the daughter of the miller. Her name is Isabella, and I want to make her my wife."

"Wife? You want to make a *miller's* daughter your wife? Millers are poor, you idiot! What has she got?"

"Beautiful eyes like the stars."

"Stars? They are worth nothing."

"Wonderful skin like the snow."

"Snow? That's worth even less."

And the poor Prince thought that

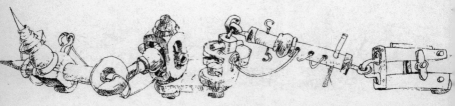

what he had loved in Isabella was the shining of her spirit by the water.

But that wouldn't do.

So he said: "She can spin straw into gold."

Well, the King was always angry, but now he was *furious*.

"Drivelling dunderhead! Nobody ever born can turn straw into gold! Get out of my sight!"

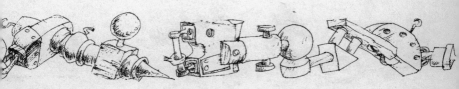

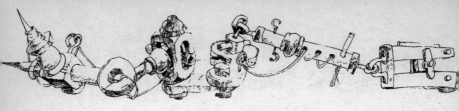

But a couple of days later, he found himself wondering. He was drinking a cup of horrible wine, because he was too mean to have anything nicer.

And he wondered.

He wondered over his horrible wine.

Straw into gold, straw into gold.

The idea was quite ridiculous, of course. But just *supposing...*

Why, he would have more gold than there was water in the sea!

He sent for his nastiest servant, a man named Grinling. The hairs that grew in Grinling's ears stood out about a foot on either side.

"Grinling," said the King, "go through the forest. Get to the riverside. Find there the beautiful daughter of a miller. Her name is Isabella."

"Yes, your majesty."

"Yes indeed, Grinling. And Grinling?"

"Yes, your majesty?"

"Bring her back before nightfall. Or else I'll grind your bones into wine!"

So Grinling didn't take long to

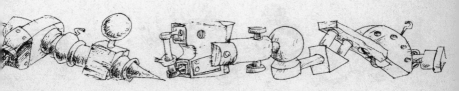

find Isabella. He dragged her back, and the old miller stood weeping on the bank, knowing he'd told a lie.

For of course Isabella couldn't spin straw into gold, any more than she could spin gold into straw. She loved her father dearly, but how she wished he hadn't been so rash! Now she was frightened to say she could, and frightened to say she couldn't.

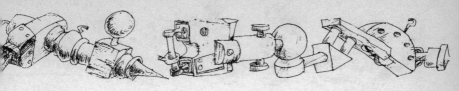

The crafty old eyes of the King were each like the tongue of a snake.

"So you are Isabella. Well, I see you are as beautiful as they say."

He sniggered.

"But beauty is quite useless, my dear. Quite useless. It won't even save your life!"

And he laughed loud and long, so his belly shook.

Now his eyes were burning.

"I understand you have a remarkable gift. We are going to put it to the test. Aren't we, Grinling?"

And Grinling, who was skulking

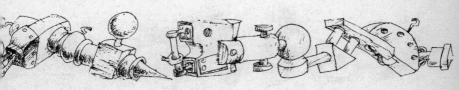

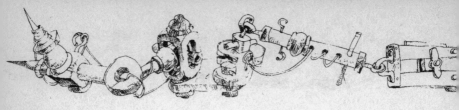

by the side of the throne, said, "Yes indeed, your majesty!"

"Yes indeed, Grinling. Now, my dear. If you can do what they say you can do, well and good. And if you can't, well ... *not so good*."

And the King spread out his hand like a blade and drew it across his throat.

"Do I make myself clear?"

Isabella trembled.

"Spin straw into gold by morning, and you shall marry my son. Fail and I fear, my dear..."

His shoulders wobbled, his mouth

twitched.

"Fail, and I fear, my dear ... you won't be marrying anyone ever at all! Take her away, Grinling!"

And as she was led up the stone stairway, the last sound Isabella heard was the King, howling and hooting and shrieking with laughter on his throne.

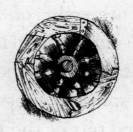

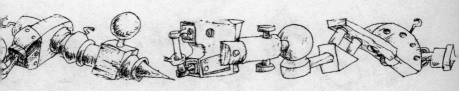

She looked round the room where Grinling had locked her. There was a stool, a spinning wheel, and a huge pile of straw.

The spinning wheel reminded her of the great mill wheel at home, that dipped and plunged and rolled in the rolling water. How happy she had been with her silly old father!

And she thought of the day the Prince came riding by. He was handsome. He was kind. And she had fallen in love with his spirit, shining by the water.

She looked out of the window.

It was miles to the ground.

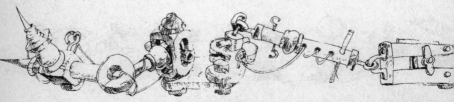

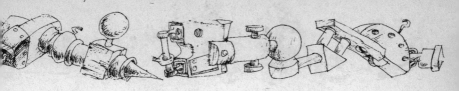

And she couldn't spin straw into anything!

She plunged her head in her hands and wept bitterly.

Then she heard a creak. She looked up. Outside the window was a high oak tree with spreading branches. And on one of them stood the strangest creature Isabella had ever seen.

It was a little man. He'd a head like a knobbly potato … and huge feet!

"Do not cry, little maiden," he said, in a voice like two rough stones being scraped against each other. "Open the window."

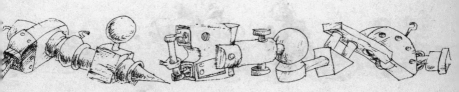

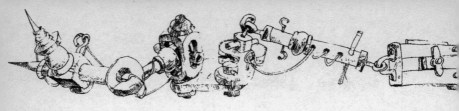

Poor Isabella had nothing to lose. So she did as he said.

He jumped on to the window ledge and down into the room.

"Well, little maiden. Things don't look very promising."

She stared at him.

"I rather think they want you to spin that pile of straw into gold by the morning. Am I right?"

"How did you know?"

"I know everything," said the little man.

"Who are you?"

"Ah! Now that would be telling!"

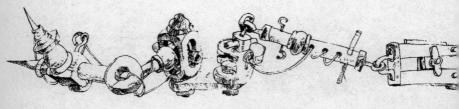

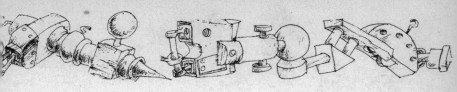

And he laughed louder than you would have thought that such a small creature could.

"It doesn't seem funny to *me*," said Isabella, and began to weep again.

"Do not cry, little maiden, do not cry. I am here to help you."

"How can you do that? Nobody can!"

"I'll spin your straw into gold. But nothing comes for nothing, little maiden. What will you give me to do it?"

"I've nothing to give you!"

"How about your necklace?"

And Isabella's hand flew to her

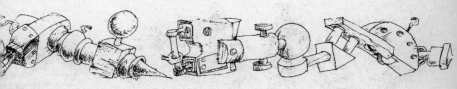

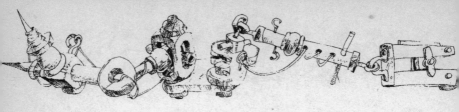

throat. Her necklace was the only gift her poor father had been able to give her. It made her sad to think of losing it. And she didn't really believe that the little man could help her. But she had no choice.

"I will give you my necklace."

"Done."

And with one of his huge and hairy feet, the little man took a tremendous BOOT at the spinning wheel!

Goodness, how he could kick!

The wheel went hurtling round. It rocked and swayed on its base, then settled into a whirr. It spun so fast

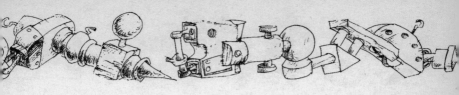

that it didn't seem to be moving at all!
And on the other side of the straw, a
river of gold came pouring down till a
great yellow mountain rose against
the wall.

Solid gold!

"Oh thank you, thank you, thank
you!" cried Isabella.

But the little man had his hand out.

She gave him the necklace.

Then she turned again to look at
the glinting treasure.

"How did you —"

But he had gone.

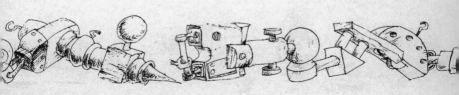

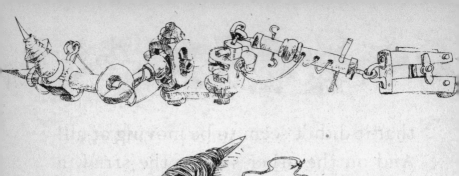

So when the King and Grinling burst into the room in the morning, they were amazed.

"This is a *fine* day, Grinling!"

"Yes, your majesty."

"Yes indeed, Grinling! Run and get me a giant cup of my bonemeal wine to celebrate! For I shall be the richest man there has ever been in the world!"

When they were down in the hall, Isabella said:

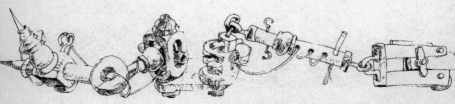

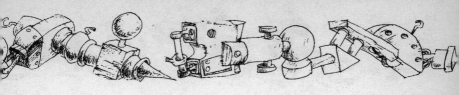

"Can I please marry the Prince now? I've done everything you wanted, your majesty."

"Ah. Well. *Ah*."

And the King's crafty old eyes were like the tongues of snakes.

Grinling stood and waggled the hair in his ears.

"My dear, that was all very well as far as it went," said the King. "Indeed, it was quite impressive. But how do we know it wasn't a flash in the pan? You must do it again tonight, and *then* you shall marry my son!"

And again Isabella was locked in

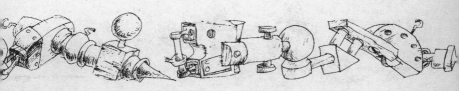

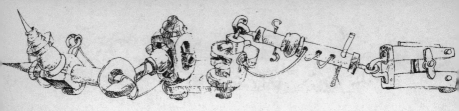

the room with the spinning wheel, the
stool, and an even bigger pile of straw.

Again she plunged her head into
her hands and bitterly she wept.

Outside a great wind was blowing.
The oak tree shivered and rocked as
though it would take off from the
ground! She looked up and she saw a
big dark bird flapping towards her in
the mighty wind. And it landed on

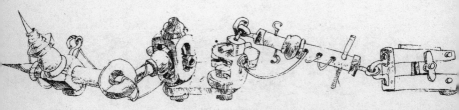

the window ledge.

But it wasn't a bird ... it was the little man!

"Do not cry, little maiden, do not cry. Open the window."

And when he was inside, he said, "All to do again I see, little maiden! What will you give me this time? For nothing comes for nothing."

"But I have nothing to give you!"

"What about your ring?"

And Isabella rubbed the ring on her finger. It had been her mother's, and it was the only thing she had left to remember her by. She would be sad

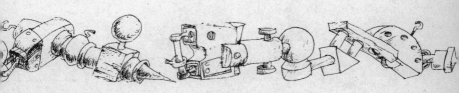

to lose it. But she had no choice.

"I will give you my ring."

"Done!"

And with one of his huge, hairy feet he took a tremendous BOOT at the spinning wheel!

Again the river of gold poured down and the yellow mountain rose from the floor.

"Oh, thank you, thank you, thank you!" cried Isabella.

But the little man had his hand out.

She gave him the ring.

He was gone.

Well, the King was even more delight-
ed when he burst in with Grinling in
the morning.

"Can I please marry the Prince
now?" said Isabella.

"Ah," said the King. "*Ah*. Now, all
the best things come in threes, my
dear. That makes them true. And just
to make sure you haven't been lucky
twice … do it again tonight! And *then*
you shall marry my son."

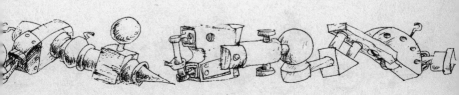

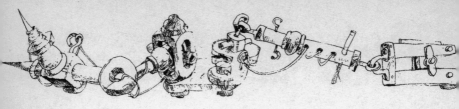

And they locked her in ... with a pile of straw so big it almost filled the room!

That night a terrible storm shook the palace. Thunder boomed and bellowed, lightning zig-zagged down the sky. But Isabella kept the window open, hoping the little man would come again.

And he did, sliding right into the room down a ladder of lightning.

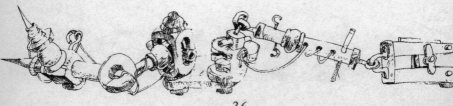

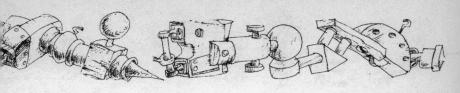

"I've *nothing* to give you this time," cried Isabella, "nothing at all!"

"But you will have, little maiden. Oh, you will have."

"What do you mean?"

"You will marry your handsome Prince."

"How do you know?"

"I know everything. And after a time your first child will be born. But…"

And the little man gave a rasping laugh from his knobbly potato head.

"You won't have it for long. You'll give it to *me*!"

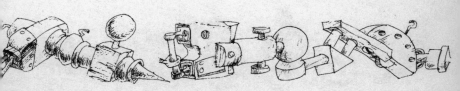

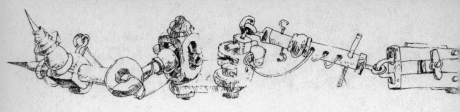

Isabella stared at him.

"I gave you my necklace, I gave you my ring ... you cannot take my child!"

"Nothing comes for nothing, little maiden. You have no choice."

And she didn't.

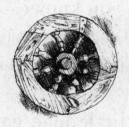

In the morning there stood the glittering yellow mountain.

And this time the King did set her

free. He felt he was sure of being the richest man there had ever been in the world!

And Isabella married the Prince. They had a wonderful wedding in the mountains. After a time their first child was born. And they were very happy.

They didn't have to worry about the King. He spent all day and night in his store-room, running his fingers over and over the shining piles of gold. He howled and hooted and shrieked with laughter, drinking cup after cup of his horrible bonemeal wine. One

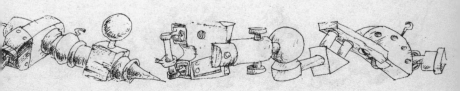

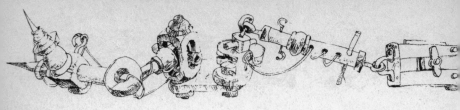

day he exploded, and that was the end of him.

But, of course, they had someone to fear.

And sure enough, one night he came.

And this time he didn't jump off a tree, or fly like a bird, or slide down a ladder of lightning. He walked on his huge feet up the stone stairway, slowly into the room where Isabella was rocking her baby in the cradle.

"Give me your child."

"Oh please," said Isabella, "please!"

And she wept twice as bitterly as she had ever wept in her life.

A funny look came over the little man's knobbly potato face. He grinned, and then he laughed with his rasping laugh.

"All right, I'll give you a chance. That might be fun!"

"What do you mean?"

"This. If you can discover my name within three days, then you shall keep your child. If not ... well, of course ... *not!*"

And he was gone.

Well, of course Isabella told her

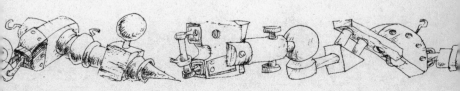

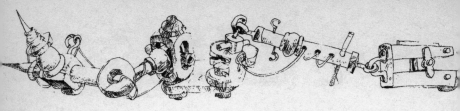

husband everything, and he was very sad.

What could they do?

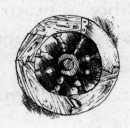

The Prince summoned the palace knights. Their names were these: Ronald the Bold, Vernon the Bald, Sidney the Big and Denzil the Bigger.

And they were as lazy and useless a bunch as you could hope to find.

"We have three days," said the

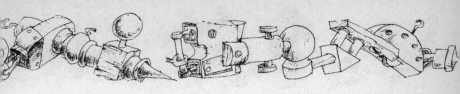

Prince, "to find out the little man's name. And that means finding *him*. Ride up into the mountains. Ride out into the forest. Go far and wide, search high and low, and bring me back his name."

"You can count on me," said Ronald the Bold.

"Consider it done," said Vernon the Bald.

"Just leave it to us," said Sidney the Big and Denzil the Bigger.

It was winter now. In the freezing wind the trees were heavily piled with snow and the paths were coated with

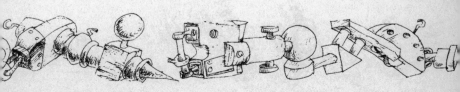

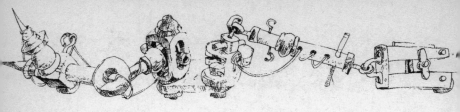

tongues of ice.

The knights were not enjoying themselves at all. They soon decided they'd had enough, so they made for a woodman's abandoned hut and sat there playing cards all day.

"We'll just make up some names," said Vernon the Bald.

And they all agreed. So that evening they told them to the Prince, who told them to Isabella.

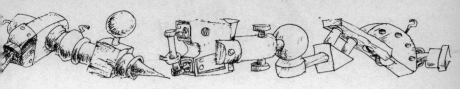

Late that night, she felt the stone stairs shudder with the little man's footsteps.

"Well? And what is my name?"

"Is it Boris?"

"It is not."

"Is it Bernard Belvedere?"

"It is not."

"Is it Brian Broderick Brewhouse Baraimian?"

"No!" cried the little man, "it is none of those things!"

And he laughed, loud and harsh.

"You will never guess it! Two nights more, and the child in that

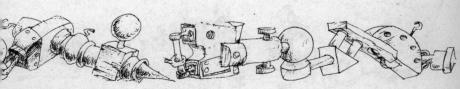

cradle is *mine*!"

He was gone.

And Isabella wept.

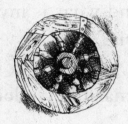

The next day the knights didn't bother to look at all. They took some bottles of the King's bonemeal wine and headed straight for the woodman's hut.

"My goodness, this wine is horrible," said Ronald.

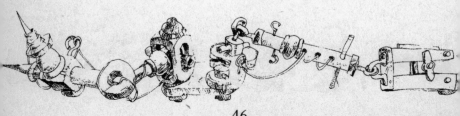

"No wonder the King was so nasty," said Vernon.

"No wonder he exploded," said Sidney and Denzil.

And they made up some more names.

The Prince told them to Isabella.

Late that night, there was the little man.

"Well, can you tell me my name?"

"Is it Peveril?"

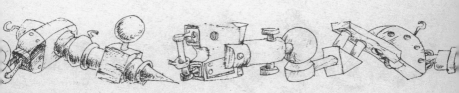

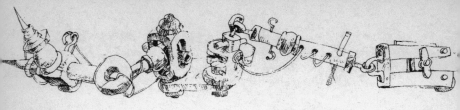

"It is not."

"Is it Peregrine Pighurst?"

"It is not."

"Is it Patrick Prendergast Petunia Junior?"

"No, it is none of those stupid, ridiculous names."

And this time he didn't laugh. The eyes in his knobbly potato face were as hard as the ice outside the palace walls.

"This is no game. Tomorrow night you will look your last on your child."

He was gone.

And bitterly, bitterly, Isabella wept.

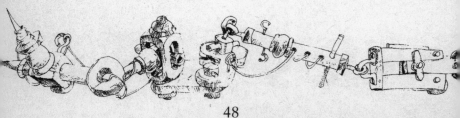

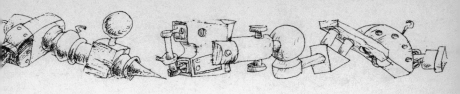

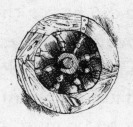

The next day was the last day.

The knights did nothing.

But three men never gave up, as the whirling flakes fell thicker than ever. One was, of course, the Prince. He rode like the wind under the mountain overhangs, white horse like a snowstorm in a snowstorm. They staggered on through the deepest drifts and they crept up icy ledges.

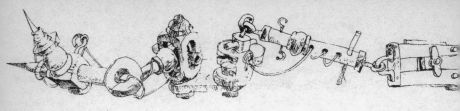

But nowhere did he see the little man, or hear any word of him.

The second was the old miller, who loved his daughter more than the breath in his body, more than his own life. He wanted to save her child. Of course he lived in the palace now, and the great mill wheel stood rusting in the frozen river. He trudged along the silent bank, hoping to hear some word of the little man. But no one he ever saw knew anything at all.

And there was a third.

This was a man who had loved Isabella from the very first moment he

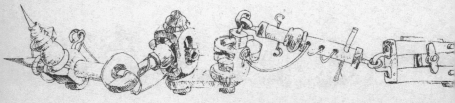

saw her. And he had hurt her.

He didn't want that. He wanted her to be happy. When at last she married the Prince, the man had been overjoyed. And now he was crawling and scrambling through thorns and undergrowth, through brambles and whipping bushes. His skin bled and his eyes stung as he looked for the little man.

Do you know who it was?

It was…

GRINLING!

For Grinling wasn't a bad person at all. Early in his life, he'd been

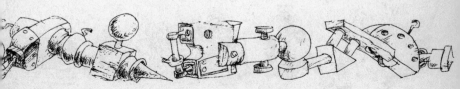

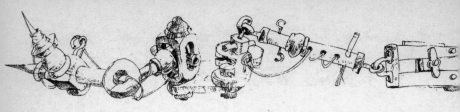

captured by the King, who made him his slave. He'd always had hairy ears, of course, but the King had made him grow them out for ever, like sideways horns. Or else he'd grind poor Grinling's bones into wine.

And he heard someone singing.

A harsh, low, rasping song, such as he'd never heard in all of his life.

He crept behind a tree.

He felt the touch of hands on his back. But he knew they were friendly. He knew they were the old hands of the miller, and the young hands of the Prince.

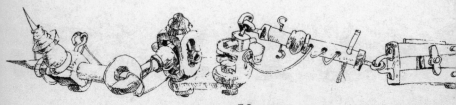

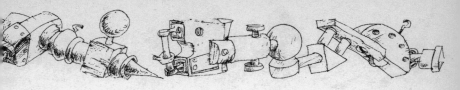

No one dared breathe.

Down in a clearing of the forest, a fire was burning brightly. And round and round it danced none other than the little man!

As he danced he sang:

"Crackle, logs, and stars, be dumb,
Tonight a royal child will come.
They'll never beat me at my game,
For RUMPELSTILTSKIN is my name!"

Softly the three watchers stole away through the snow.

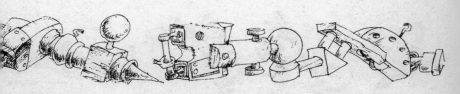

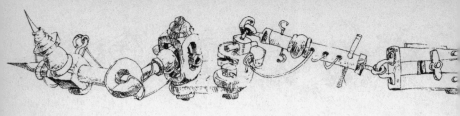

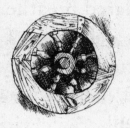

That night, everyone in the palace was waiting and whispering, when they felt the shudder of footsteps on the stairway.

"Well?" said the little man.

"Oh," said Isabella. "It's you again. Now, tell me. Could your name be Tim?"

"It is not," he sneered.

"Is it Jim?"

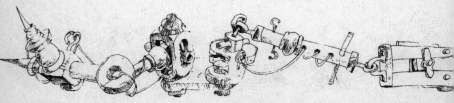

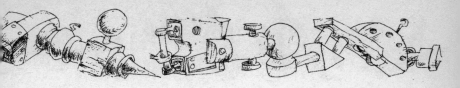

"It is not."

And this time he grinned from ear to ear.

"Oh well, then," said Isabella, gently rocking the cradle with her foot, "I suppose it must be Rumpelstiltskin."

The little man's face froze like the ice on the mountains. Then it split in a great bellow of rage that shook the palace walls. He lifted a huge, hairy foot and he STAMPED!

He stamped so hard he went through the floor, and through the floor under that, and through the basement. He stamped so hard he

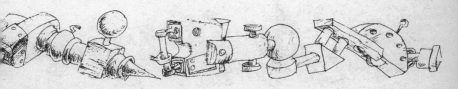

went down, down, down, to the centre of the earth. And nobody ever saw him again.

The Prince and Isabella had many more children. On summer days, they walk with them through the forest and down to the riverside. The great mill wheel is again turning, for the lazy knights have to work there by the water.

The cogs creak, and the shaft

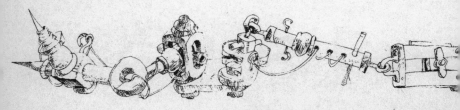

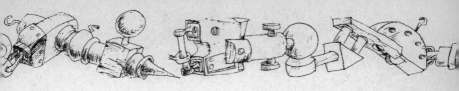

spins, and the great stone goes grinding round.

It's like an elephant dancing ... for
joy!

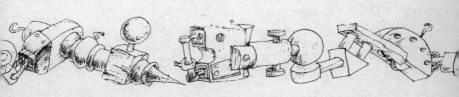

Other stories to collect:

Aesop's Fables

Malorie Blackman
Illustrated by Patrice Aggs

Once upon a time there was a man named Aesop
who told stories full of wisdom…

Hansel and Gretel

Henrietta Branford
Illustrated by Lesley Harker

Once upon a time there were a brother and sister
who were left alone in the forest…

The Snow Queen

Berlie Doherty

Illustrated by Siân Bailey

Once upon a time there was a little boy whose
heart was turned to ice…

The Twelve
Dancing Princesses

Anne Fine

Illustrated by Debi Gliori

Once upon a time there were twelve princesses,
and no one knew why their shoes were full
of holes…

Grey Wolf, Prince Jack and the Firebird

Alan Garner

Illustrated by James Mayhew

Once upon a time there was a prince who set out
to seek the mysterious firebird...

Mossycoat

Philip Pullman

Illustrated by Peter Bailey

Once upon a time there was a beautiful girl whose
mother made her a magical, mossy coat...

The Six Swan Brothers

Adèle Geras

Illustrated by Ian Beck

Once upon a time there was a brave princess
who saw her six brothers turned into swans...

The Seal Hunter

Tony Mitton

Illustrated by Nick Maland

Once upon a time there was a cruel fisherman
who was dragged to the bottom of the ocean
by a seal prince...

Cockadoodle-doo, Mr Sultana!

Michael Morpurgo
Illustrated by Michael Foreman

Once upon a time there was a rich and greedy
sultan who met a clever little cockerel...

Rapunzel

Jacqueline Wilson
Illustrated by Nick Sharratt

Once upon a time there was a baby who was
stolen by a witch...

The Three Heads
in the Well

Susan Gates

Illustrated by Sue Heap

Once upon a time there were two stepsisters –
one good, one bad – who both went out to seek
their fortunes…

The Goose Girl

Gillian Cross

Illustrated by Jason Cockcroft

Once upon a time there was a princess who lost
everything she ever owned…